Sponsored Education Program

Spot

Best Friends Series
Book 2

David M. Sargent, Jr. and his friends all live in a small town in northwest Arkansas. While he lies in the hammock, the dogs (left to right: Spike, Emma, Daphne and Mary) play ball, dig holes or bark at kitty cats. When not playing in the yard, they travel around the United States, meeting children and writing stories.

Spot

Best Friends Series
Book 2

David M. Sargent, Jr.

Illustrated by Debbie Farmer

Ozark Publishing, Inc.
P.O. Box 228
Prairie Grove, AR 72753

Cataloging-in-Publication Data

Sargent, David M., 1966–
     Spot / by David M. Sargent, Jr. ;
illustrated by Debbie Farmer.—Prairie Grove, AR :
Ozark Publishing, c2007.
     p. cm. (Best friends series ; 2)

     "Helpful"—Cover.
     SUMMARY: When Spot's black nose
starts wiggling, he wakes up. Immediately,
he smells smoke! Without hesitating, the
Dalmatian goes into action!
     ISBN 1-59381-056-3 (hc)
            1-59381-057-1 (pbk)

     1. Dogs—Juvenile fiction.
[1. Dogs—Fiction. 2. Dalmatian—Fiction.]
I. Farmer, Debbie, 1958– ill. II. Title.
III. Series.

     PZ8.3.S2355Sp 2007
     [E]—dc21   2003099196

iv

Inspired by

the night one of my dogs woke me up from a deep sleep. Gas was leaking from my stove.

Dedicated to

all children who have Dalmatians.

Foreword

When Spot's black nose starts wiggling, he wakes up. Immediately, he smells smoke! Without hesitating, the Dalmatian goes into action!

Contents

If you would like to have the author of the Best Friends Series visit your school free of charge, please call 1-800-321-5671.

One

Smoke!

Spot was dreaming of a big, juicy bone that Suzie was handing to him. He drooled and licked his lips. Suddenly the dream faded. He sat up and wiggled his nose.

Spot knew that something was wrong. He looked toward the house and whined. It was the middle of the night. His master's house was dark. Once again, he sniffed the air with his black nose. *Smoke!*

The Dalmatian leaped to his feet. Barking frantically, he raced up the steps of the porch, but no one came to the door.

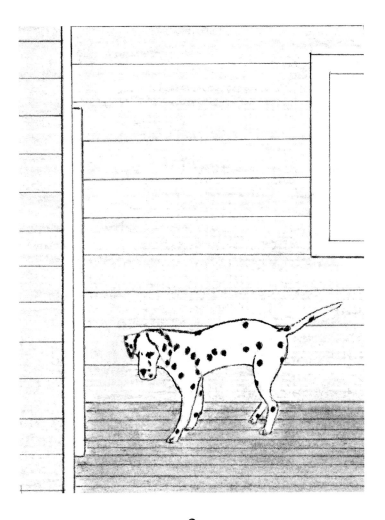

He quickly glanced up at Suzie's bedroom, but she was not standing at the window. His heart pounded with fear as he raced around the house to try to awaken his family.

A moment later, flames licked the air above the roof of the house. Spot found an open window, and his paws crashed against the screen. Biting and clawing his way through the woven metal, he climbed inside.

He crashed into the living room. He leaped to his feet. His dark eyes burned from the smoke as he reached the landing. He hurried to his little master's bedroom.

Little Suzie was sound asleep when Spot arrived at her bedside. He put his front paw on her arm and barked. The little girl did not wake up. His damp tongue licked her face as he pawed the blankets.

"Spot! What are you doing in my room? You are not supposed to be in the house," Suzie whispered. "What is the matter with you? Bad dog!"

Two

The House Is on Fire!

Suddenly Suzie realized that the room was filling with smoke.

Suzie coughed and said, "Fire! You are trying to tell me the house is on fire! Good dog, Spot!"

Tears rolled down her cheeks as she ran to her little brother's room.

"Billy," she yelled. "Get up! The house is on fire!"

Suzie grabbed her little brother by the hand. He was three years old. As she pulled him out of bed, he began to cry.

Spot barked loudly as he led Suzie and Billy from the smoky room.

"Mama! I want my mama!" Billy
screamed.

Spot ran to Suzie's mama and daddy's bedroom. Spot met them at the door. They had been awakened by his barking and the cries of their children.

The crackle of burning wood and falling timbers filled the upstairs. The Dalmatian carefully led Suzie and her family down the stairs and to the front door.

Three

A Dalmatian Hero

Later, Spot sat quietly beside the big red fire truck. Suzie stood beside him.

They watched as the firemen gathered up their hoses and all of their fire-fighting equipment.

"You have a fine dog, Suzie," the Fire Chief said. Your father tells me that your Dalmatian, Spot, saved everyone's life."

"Yessir," Suzie said. "Spot saved us. He woke me up. Then we got my little brother up."

"I see," the Fire Chief said.

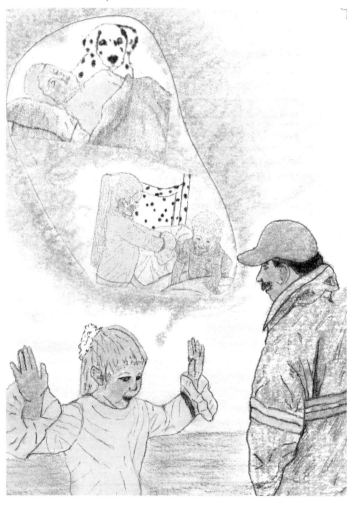

"Then Spot went to Mama and Daddy's room," Suzie continued. "He led Mama, Daddy, Billy and me out of the house."

Suzie hugged the Dalmatian. "You saved our lives, Spot!"

"Spot would make a great fire station dog," the Fire Chief said.

"Oh no, sir," Suzie said in a proud voice. "But he can visit you anytime. Spot stays with me! I love him. He's my best friend."